ICKY R... 5

THE TWO-DOLLAR DiRT SHiRT

BUZZZZZZ

BUZZZZZZ

BUZZZZZZ

Written & illustrated by

MICHAEL REX

A STEPPING STONE BOOK™

Random House 🏠 New York

To Hank, for showing me the money

All rights reserved. Published in the United States by Random House Children's Books, a division of Penguin Random House LLC, New York.

Random House and the colophon are registered trademarks and A Stepping Stone Book and the colophon are trademarks of Penguin Random House LLC.

Visit us on the Web!
SteppingStonesBooks.com
randomhousekids.com

Educators and librarians, for a variety of teaching tools, visit us at RHTeachersLibrarians.com

Library of Congress Cataloging-in-Publication Data
Rex, Michael, author, illustrator.
The two-dollar dirt shirt / written & illustrated by Michael Rex.
p. cm. — (Icky Ricky ; 5)
"A Stepping Stone Book."
Summary: "Ricky makes a shirt out of dirt and gets into plenty of trouble—and mess."
—Provided by publisher.
ISBN 978-0-385-37559-7 (pbk.) — ISBN 978-0-385-37560-3 (lib. bdg.) —
ISBN 978-0-385-37561-0 (ebook)
[1. Behavior—Fiction. 2. Humorous stories.] I. Title.
PZ7.R32875Tw 2015 [E]—dc23 2014011110

Printed in the United States of America
10 9 8 7 6 5 4 3 2 1

This book has been officially leveled by the F&P Text Level Gradient™ Leveling System.

CONTENTS

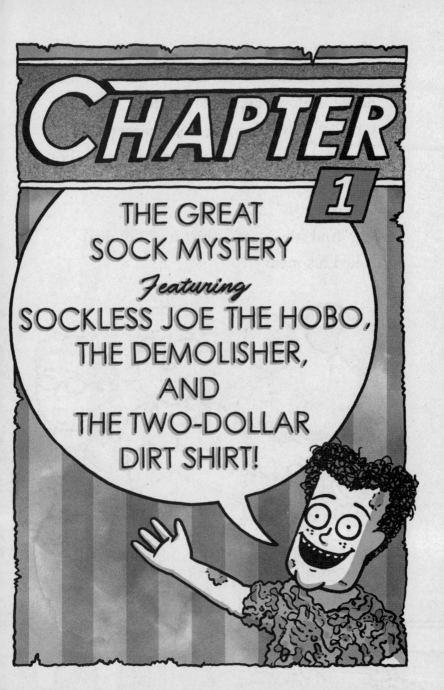

"Surprise!" yelled a crowd of people as Icky Ricky walked through the front door of his house. Before they could all shout "Happy birthday," Ricky's mom stopped them.

"Ricky! Is your shirt made of dirt?" she asked.

"Yes it is," said Ricky.

"And why is your shirt made of dirt?" asked his mom.

"Because I couldn't find Sockless Joe
the Hobo," said Ricky.

"All right," said Ricky's mom. "Tell
us everything." She pulled up a chair and
sat down. Everyone in the room looked at
Ricky.

"Sure," said Ricky. "This is what
happened. . . ."

HAPPY BIRTHDAY!

$2.00

It all started when Stew and Gus and I were crossing the street. There was a sock right in the middle of it.

I was like, "Hey, some dude lost his sock!" and I picked it up.

"How could you lose a sock?" asked Stew.

"Maybe he was driving along and said, 'I don't want to wear socks today.' Then he just threw it out the window," I said.

"Or maybe it was too hot," said Gus. "And he just had to take it off."

"Maybe he was a really cool guy and was like, 'Man, socks are for losers!' and tossed it out the window," said Stew.

"And it went right into the window of another car!" I said.

"Ha! Imagine that!" said Stew. "You're driving along, and a sock comes flying in the window."

"Yeah," said Gus. "You'd probably crash your car and be really mad."

"But what if you were late for work and you only had time to put on one sock, and then a sock came flying in the window?" I asked.

"You'd be like, 'Awesome!'" said Stew.

"Or if it didn't fit, you'd just chuck it out *your* window!" said Gus.

"You know," I said, "if your sock fell off, then your shoe would have to fall off as well."

"Yeah," said Gus. "You'd have to lose a shoe, too."

"Yeah, and then you'd have a bare foot all day," said Stew.

"And then you would get to work and you would get fired because you were missing a shoe," I said.

"Then you'd get really poor," said Stew.

"And become a hobo!" said Gus.

"Sockless Joe the Hobo!" I said, and we all started cracking up.

Then I had my best idea of the day!

"We should find out who this belongs to!" I said. "We'll go door-to-door and find out who lost this sock so he doesn't have to become a hobo!"

"Like Cinderella," said Stew.

"Sockerella," said Gus.

We went to the first house. "Did you lose a sock?" I asked the man who opened the door.

"No, sorry," said the man. "But I did lose a watch a couple of years ago. If you find that, let me know."

At the next house, a lady answered the door.

"Did you lose a sock?" I asked.

I held it up to show her. Her face got all scrunchy, and she held her nose.

"Even if I did, I wouldn't want it back," said the lady.

We tried house after house. No one
had lost a sock, but lots of people told us
to clean our hands with sanitizer. The next
house we went to was all boarded up, and
there was a backhoe parked on the little
lawn. But there were no workers around.

"I wonder what's going on here," I said,
and we walked up the front steps. There
were some papers taped to the front door,
and they all said stuff like "Condemned"
and "Demolish."

"Cool," said Stew. "They're gonna demolish this house."

"Yeah," said Gus. "I want to see that."

"That would be such a cool job!" I said. "I'd call myself Ricky the Demolisher! And I'd work on Saturdays and Sundays, too."

We looked around the back of the house and noticed that the garage door was open.

"Maybe Sockless Joe lives in there," I said. We walked to the garage.

"You sure we should be here?" asked Gus.

"It might be private property," said Stew.

"No one lives here, and they're gonna smash the place," I said. "It should be fine."

It was an old garage with a dirt floor. It had all been cleaned out except for one box that said "Garage Sale" on it. There wasn't much in the box. Some plastic forks, a frame with no picture, a can of old hair spray, and a little paper tag that said "$2.00." I picked up the hair spray.

"I wonder if it's full," I said, and sprayed some on my arm. It was kinda sticky.

Gus picked up the tag and held it on his finger. "Hey! Look at me! I'm two dollars."

Stew and I laughed.

"That's a rip-off!" I said.

"I'd only pay fifty cents for a Gus!" said Stew.

I took the tag and put it on the sock. "Maybe we can sell this!" I said.

"Who's gonna buy one sock for two dollars?" asked Stew.

"Someone with only one sock," I said.

We heard an engine, and we looked out of the garage. A bunch of construction guys in a pickup truck turned off the street into the driveway. We panicked!

There was a really skinny door in the
back of the garage. We all tried to run
through it at once, but we got stuck. Gus
and Stew popped out first, and then I
pushed through.

My shirt got caught on some nail heads that were sticking out along the side of the door. I pulled really hard, and my shirt ripped. I twisted out of my shirt and ran.

Behind the garage were a couple of trees and a low fence. We hopped over the fence and hid. The ground was dry, and the dirt was all dusty.

"Why did we run away?" asked Stew.

"You said it was okay for us to be there," said Gus.

"Well, I wasn't positive," I said. "We might have gotten in trouble. I just didn't want to find out."

"Where's your shirt?" asked Gus.

I told them.

"Do you need to go back and get it?" asked Stew.

"No," I said. "It's all ripped."

"You'll need a shirt if we want to sell that sock," said Stew.

"I thought we were going to find the owner," said Gus.

"Either way, you're going to need a shirt when you go home," Stew said.

"Hey, look," said Gus. He pointed to my arm where I'd sprayed the hair spray. Dirt had stuck to it. Then I had my best idea of the day!

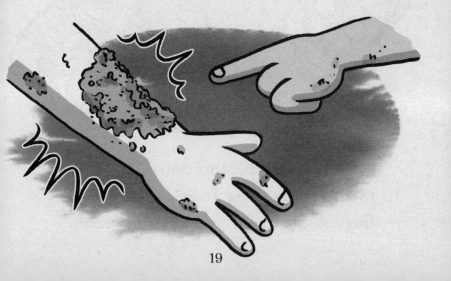

"We can make a shirt!" I said. "Spray me everywhere a shirt would be." Gus sprayed my chest, my stomach, my back, and the tops of my arms.

Then I rolled around in the dirt. When I stood up, it looked perfect!

"Presenting the Dirt Shirt!" I said, and I walked around like I was a supermodel. Gus and Stew pretended to take pictures.

The two-dollar tag had gotten stuck to my side. We started walking home, and I showed the Dirt Shirt to everyone I could find.

"Step right up and get your Dirt Shirt! Only two dollars!" I said. "That's right! Only two smackers!"

"And that's why I'm wearing a dirt shirt," said Ricky to his mom.

"I see," said Ricky's mom. "Happy birthday!" she added.

Everyone in the room followed along. "Happy birthday!" they all cheered.

"I'd hug you if your shirt wasn't made of dirt," said Ricky's mom.

"That's okay!" said Ricky. He laughed and asked his mom, "How'd you get everyone here without me seeing?"

"Well, at first we were going to have someone take you to a movie or something," she said. "But Gus and Stew said they would keep you busy."

"I put an old sock in the road," said Ricky's dad, "because I knew you would spend hours trying to figure out where it came from, or building something with it."

Ricky laughed again. "Here. You can have it back." He took the sock from his pocket and handed it to his dad.

"This isn't the sock I put out," said his dad as he scratched his chin. "We need to find out where this came from! Let's go, boys!"

ICKY RICKY'S

PARTY GAMES!

Birthday parties can be lots of fun, especially if you play the right games. Here are some ideas for your next super-fun bash!

#1: Something Strange Is in My Belly

Put strange objects under your shirt. Have your fellow partygoers try to guess what they are. The closest guess wins!

#2: Jelly Puzzle

Put the pieces of a small puzzle in a full jar of jelly. The first person to pull out all the pieces and put the puzzle together wins!

#3: Musical Gus

Play music. When the music stops, sit on Gus. Everyone wins!

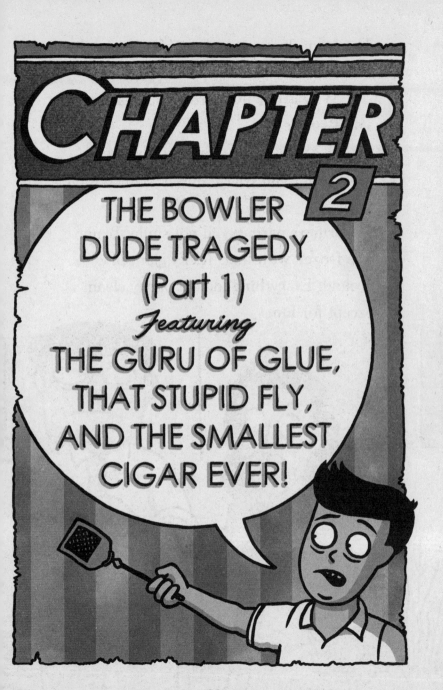

The front door opened, and Ricky watched as Bruno's parents walked in.

"Why is our living room such a mess?" said Bruno's dad.

"Because we couldn't find the teeny-tiny cigar," said Ricky, and he smiled a big smile.

Bruno's parents did not smile. Bruno was frozen with fear. Ricky glanced around. Everything looked pretty clean, except for him.

"Is your name Ricky?" asked Bruno's dad, still not smiling.

"It sure is," said Ricky.

"What's that thing on the coffee table?" asked Bruno's mom.

"Oh, that! That's all my fault," said Ricky. "I'll tell you what happened. . . ."

It all started when Bruno and I
were assigned to work on a book report
together. I would have liked to work with
one of my best friends, Gus or Stew, but
you have to work with the person you're
told to work with. So Bruno invited
me over.

When I got here, Bruno was flipping out because he'd broken this valuable antique statue.

"Dude, how did that happen?" I asked.

"I was chasing a fly around the house trying to kill it. It landed on the statue, and I just swatted it really hard. The swatter knocked the statue from the shelf, and it broke into a thousand pieces!"

I looked at the ground, and there
weren't really a thousand pieces, more like
twenty or thirty, which was a good thing.

I CAN FIX IT! DO YOU HAVE ANY
GLUE? I'M THE GURU OF GLUE!

"What the heck's a guru?" asked
Bruno.

"An expert!" I told him. "So, do you
have any glue?"

"Yeah," he said. "I'll go get it."

"Great," I said. "I'll start picking up
the pieces." I got down on my knees and
carefully picked up the pieces and put them
on the coffee table.

Bruno ran back into the room.

"Not on the good coffee table!" he screamed. "It'll get scratched, and my parents will kill me!"

So I pulled the front of my shirt up like a shelf and put the pieces there.

"How's this glue?" he asked. It was white kiddie glue.

"Not that!" I said. "Do you have any really strong stuff? It usually comes in a little tiny tube."

"I'll look," said Bruno. Then he asked, "What are we going to do about the book report?"

"I'll start gluing this, and you can start the report," I said.

"Okay," he said, and he ran off to look for glue.

I started to figure out which pieces fit with each other. Some were easy, but some I couldn't figure out at all.

Bruno ran back into the living room with a small tube of Gargantuan Glue.

"Whoa!" I said. "This is heavy-duty stuff." I looked at the label, and it had all these warnings:

"Darn! I really wanted to eat some of this glue," I said. I pretended to chug it.

"This isn't funny, Ricky!" said Bruno. "My parents are going to be home in forty-five minutes. We gotta fix this thing."

"Okay!" I said. I uncapped the glue and started to squeeze it out onto the pieces that fit together.

"Wait! Wait!" Bruno yelled. "Let me get some newspaper so the glue doesn't drip on anything." He ran off to the kitchen and came back with a pile of newspapers and put them everywhere. He put them on the table, on the floor around the table, on the couch next to the table. He even put some on the chair all the way across the room.

"I don't think the glue is going to get over there!" I said.

"That's a designer chair! We can't take chances," he said.

Once he was done, I was about to start again.

"Wait!" he shouted.

I stopped what I was doing.

He got up and ran into the kitchen and came back with two big garbage bags.

"We should wear these so we don't get glue on our clothes," he said. He tore some holes in his bag and put it on like a smock. I kept matching up pieces of the statue while he did this.

"Aren't you going to put yours on?" he asked.

"Uh, no," I said. I was already holding a bunch of pieces together, and they would have all fallen apart if I let go to put the bag on. "I think I'll glue better without it."

"But you'll get glue on your clothes, then you might stick to other things, and then I'll get in more trouble, and then—"

I cut him off. "Bruno," I said. "Let me do the gluing, and you can do the book reporting."

"Okay! Okay!" said Bruno.

I started gluing the pieces, but some just didn't fit.

"Hey, Bruno?" I asked. "I can't figure out how this goes together. What did it look like before it got busted?"

"It's an old guy holding a bowling ball," he said. Then he stood up. "He looks like this." Then he posed.

"Oh yeah," said Bruno. "He's smoking a cigar."

"Really?" I asked. "An old guy with a cigar? I'll call him the Stogie Fogey." I started cracking up, but Bruno wasn't laughing at all. "It really must be old, then, because no one smokes cigars anymore."

The statue started coming together, but some big pieces were missing.

Bruno looked at it. "Where's the cigar?" he asked.

"I don't know," I told him.

We got down on our knees where the Stogie Fogey had broken. There were still lots of tiny pieces that I couldn't glue together at all.

"Where's the dumb cigar?" asked Bruno as he looked all over.

"We gotta find that micro-stogie!"
I yelled.

Bruno smiled for the first time.

I called out like I was looking for a dog,
"Here, micro-stogie, stogie, stogie!"

Bruno started laughing. A clock in the
corner bonged a few times.

Bruno looked up. He stopped laughing.
"My parents will be home in thirty
minutes!"

TO BE CONTINUED . . .

"Ricky!" said Dr. Henderson, the school principal. "What happened to Gus?"

"He's asleep," said Ricky. He and Stew were dragging a snoozing Gus into the cafeteria.

"Why is he asleep?" asked the principal.

"Because his mom makes the best cookies ever," said Ricky.

"I can't even begin to know what that means," said Dr. Henderson. Then he looked closer at Ricky. "Why are you wet and covered with mustard?"

"I may have eaten too many hamburgers," said Ricky.

Dr. Henderson crossed his arms and gave Ricky a serious look.

"Let me explain, okay?" said Ricky. . . .

It all started at five o'clock, when I came back to school for International Food Night. I walked through the cafeteria, where everyone was setting up their food. Everything smelled really good. I looked around and found my space. There was a sign there that said "International Food Night Presents: Hot Dogs."

A few kids came up and read the sign. One kid was like, "Hot dogs aren't international."

"Yeah," said another kid, "they're American."

"That's why I made them," I said.

"But you're supposed to make a food from the country that your family comes from," said another kid.

"My parents consider our family American," I told them, "because my great-great-grandparents were born here."

One of the kids looked at my space again. "But where are the hot dogs?"

"I'm going to get them now," I said, and I ran from the cafeteria.

Earlier that day when I came to school, I had brought fifty hot dogs and my mom's slow cooker. I had put water in the slow cooker and turned it on and let it sit in Ms. Jay's class all day. That's the best way to make hot dogs.

On the way up to my classroom, I found Gus. He had a hot dog costume on to help me promote my food. Stew was going to help by bringing the hot dog buns.

Gus is really happy anytime he can wear a costume, but he didn't look right.

"What's wrong?" I asked. "You look sick."

"My mom baked two trays of cookies for the dessert table," said Gus. "I ate a whole tray on the way over here." Gus's mom makes the best cookies ever.

"Are you gonna barf?" I asked.

"I hope not," said Gus. "Because if a food makes you barf, you can never, ever eat that food again without thinking of barfing."

"Yeah," I said. "Then you would never be able to eat your mom's cookies again." We went up to the classroom to get my hot dogs. The slow cooker wasn't hot.

"It's not on!" I said. I looked around and saw that I had never plugged it in! "They're not cooked!"

"Uh-oh," said Gus. "What are you going to do?"

I had to think fast.

"We'll bring them down to the cafeteria and plug the slow cooker in," I said.

"But won't it take time to heat up?"

"Yeah," I said. Then I had my best idea of the day. "I know! We can put it on the dessert table—that way it will be like an hour before anyone eats one! They won't be as good as when they slow-cook, but at least we can serve them."

"Sounds great," said Gus. Then he
burped, and it really smelled.

BRAAAAAP!

"Wow! That was nasty," I said. "I think
you're gonna barf."

"Stop talking about it," said Gus.

I picked up the slow cooker, and we ran out of the room and down the hall. Just as we were getting to the stairs, I tripped on the slow cooker cord. The pot flipped over, and all fifty hot dogs and the water went flying down the stairs. Gus bumped into me, and we both fell. We flipped and slid down the wet staircase, squishing hot dogs all the way.

I think Gus's puffy hot dog costume saved us. We didn't get hurt, and the slow cooker wasn't broken. Not even the lid. However, something in my backpack made a loud crack and a pop.

I had brought ketchup, mustard, relish, and sauerkraut to put on the hot dogs. I opened my backpack. The jar of relish had broken and popped the sauerkraut bag. It all came spilling out of my backpack and onto the floor.

"Oh, man, we're cursed!" said Gus.

"The Hot Dog Gods are not on our side today!" I said.

I got on my knees and started to pick up the hot dogs. I held up some crushed hot dogs above my head.

OH, GREAT GODS OF HOT DOGS! OH, POWERFUL WIENER LORDS! WHAT HAVE I DONE TO UPSET YOU? HAVE I EATEN TOO MANY TACOS? TOO MANY HAMBURGERS? HAVE I IGNORED YOUR WONDERFUL WIENERNESS FOR TOO LONG?

Gus started laughing. "'Wienerness' isn't a word."

"It is now," I said.

He laughed again and bent over and held his stomach. He stepped across the mess to lean on the wall, but his foot came down on the mustard bottle and it shot all over me.

"Sorry," said Gus.

"It's okay," I said. "It is obvious that the All-Knowing Lord of Franks has it in for me."

I knelt again, and I saw that some hot dogs had gone under a big radiator that was built into the wall. The radiator was pretty warm. Then I had my best idea of the day. On the top of the radiator, there was a little ledge. We keep our gloves there on snowy days to warm them up. I put as many hot dogs on the ledge as I could.

"I'll heat them up this way!" I said.

I got down on my belly and pulled out the hot dogs that rolled under the radiator. They were all covered with fuzz and gum and little rocks and junk, plus some of the sauerkraut and relish that had seeped across the floor.

"Wow!" I said. "It's like a secret colony of mutant hot dogs." I shook one in Gus's face.

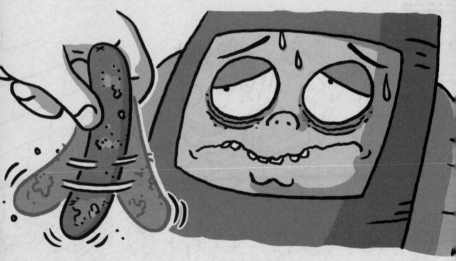

Normally he'd crack up, but this time he just turned around, ran down the hall, bent over a garbage can, and barfed into it.

I'd never seen a barfing hot dog before.

I really wanted to share my awesome
hot dogs with everyone at the school. But
I couldn't share these. I mean, I've eaten
some gross stuff, but no one else wants to
eat a hot dog cooked on a radiator.

Then Stew burst through the door.
"Guys," he said, "I've been waiting for you
in the cafeteria forever."

I told him what had happened.

"You really must be cursed," said Stew.
"Because I couldn't find any hot dog buns.
There were no more at the store, so I just
bought some loaves of white bread."

Gus walked back to us, and he looked a
little better. Barfing usually does that. He
sat down against the wall and closed his
eyes.

"I'm going to sleep," he said. He always
sleeps right after he barfs. In two seconds,
he was snoozing away.

"What are we going to do about all this?" asked Stew, and he pointed at the giant mess.

"I guess we should clean it up."

We picked up all the hot dogs and chucked them in the garbage can that Gus had barfed in. Then we dumped out everything else in my backpack into the garbage. Luckily the garbage can was on wheels, so we pushed it waaaaay down the hall because it was getting stinky.

There was still some mustard and sauerkraut on the floor, but it didn't seem as wet anymore. Then we noticed that Gus's hot dog suit was soaking up all the water.

The only things we had left that were any good were the bottle of ketchup and the loaves of bread. I also had a bag of little flags that I was going to stick in the hot dogs, to make them totally American. Then I had my best idea of the day.

"Ketchup sandwiches!" I said to
Stew. "We can make a pile of ketchup
sandwiches. They're kind of American."

"Yeah!" said Stew.

We started making sandwiches. They
looked okay, but nothing special.

"You know what would make these better?" said Stew. "If we made them triple-decker sandwiches."

"Yeah!" I said, and we went to work putting more ketchup and another slice of bread on each sandwich.

"You know what would make these even better?" I said. "If we made them six-layer sandwiches!"

Stew laughed.

We placed all the triple-deckers on all the other triple-deckers. They were looking awesome.

"Y'know," said Stew, "if we want to make them *really* American, we should make the biggest ketchup sandwich ever!"

"Everything in America is bigger!" I said.

We started piling up the six-decker sandwiches. There were eighteen slices in each loaf, so when we had them all piled up, the sandwich was thirty-six slices high. We even kept the crust-covered end pieces in there.

The sandwich wobbled a bit, but we caught it. I opened the little bag of flags, and we stuck them all over to hold it together.

"This looks great!" I said. "Let's get it out there on the table!" I tried to pick the sandwich up, but it almost fell over.

"We're not going to be able to carry it without breaking it," said Stew.

"We need a dolly to carry it on," I said.

We looked over at Gus, who was still sleeping against the wall. We both knew what to do. We scooted the sandwich over to him and leaned it against the front of his hot dog costume. I grabbed his feet and pulled him slowly from the wall. As he leaned back, Stew pushed the sandwich against him and it stayed together. It was perfect.

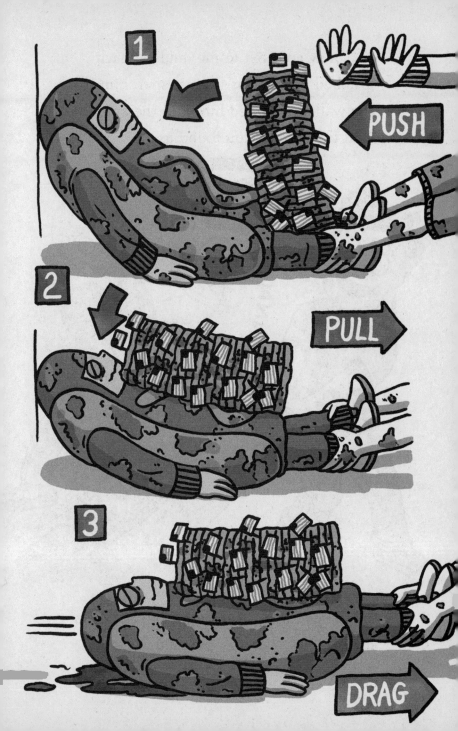

Stew got next to me, and we each grabbed one of Gus's arms, spun him from the wall, and pulled him into the cafeteria! And that's when you found us.

"I see," said Dr. Henderson. "It looks like you boys did all you could."

"We tried," said Ricky.

"Why don't you pull Gus into my office so he can get some sleep," said the principal. He walked off and picked up a cafeteria tray. Ricky and Stew pulled Gus into the hall and around a corner to the principal's office.

Dr. Henderson walked in after them and pointed to a couch. "Put him there," he said.

Ricky and Stew started to lift Gus.

"Wait," said Dr. Henderson. He held the cafeteria tray close to the ketchup sandwich tower and rolled the tower from Gus's belly onto the tray.

The boys lifted Gus and put him on the couch. He was still sleeping deeply.

"Now you boys run along and get something good to eat," said Dr. Henderson. "Go get yourself a taco or a dumpling or a samosa."

"What about you?" asked Ricky.

"I'll stay here," said Dr. Henderson, and he sat down at his desk. He placed the tray holding the ketchup sandwich tower in front of him. He reached into a desk drawer and pulled out a fork and knife.

"Why would I leave," asked Dr. Henderson, "when I can eat this entire thing all by myself?"

MORE of ICKY RICKY'S

PARTY GAMES!

#4: Closet of Terror

Have everyone take turns going into a dark closet.
Have each person scream as loud as possible.
The person who screams the longest wins.

AAAA AAAAA AAAA
AAAAAAH!

#5: Cake Finger Ninja

When no one is looking, try to scoop some icing off the birthday cake. Don't get caught! The person with the most scoops wins.

#6: Musical Gus Extreme

Play loud, fast music. When the music stops, sit on Gus really hard. Everyone wins!

UGH!

"Attack!" shouted Mean Dean as he started chucking snowballs at the strange beast running across the park. His friend Trent followed his orders and whipped his snowballs.

"Truce! Truce!" called a voice from inside the beast. "It's just me, Ricky!"

Icky Ricky poked his head out so the boys could see him. They stopped throwing snowballs.

"What the heck are you dressed as?" asked Mean Dean.

"I'm a woolly attack mammoth!" said Ricky.

"Why the heck are you a woolly attack mammoth?" asked Trent.

"Yeah," said Mean Dean. "That's kind of a stupid thing to be."

"Because I found all the fire hydrants," said Ricky.

"Is this gonna be another one of your stupid stories?" asked Mean Dean.

"It might be!" said Ricky. . . .

It all started this morning with the
snow day. Since we didn't have to go to
school, I knew it would be a good day to
make some money shoveling sidewalks and
driveways. I got all dressed up in my snow
gear, but I had so many layers on that my
coat didn't fit, so I wore one of my dad's. It
was kind of long, but it covered everything.

I grabbed a shovel and went to get
Stew and Gus. But Gus couldn't get a
shovel because his garage was locked, and
Stew could only get a little shovel that's
good for the beach.

So we rang people's doorbells and asked them if they wanted us to shovel their driveways or anything.

One man thought about it, but then he said, "There are three of you and only one shovel."

Stew showed him his little shovel, but the man just laughed.

"No thanks," said the man. "I'll do it myself."

This happened over and over, and no one hired us.

We were getting hungry and we didn't have any food with us, so we started to eat big handfuls of snow. The snow was good for packing, so we'd shape it into things we liked.

"Mine's a slice of pizza," I said.

"Mine's a hamburger," said Stew.

"Mine's a falafel!" said Gus, and we started cracking up.

SNOW PIZZA

SNOW BURGER

SNOW FALAFEL

"What the heck's a falafel?" I asked.

"A bread pocket filled with stuff like lettuce and these fried balls of chickpeas!"

"Ewwww!" I said,

"Sounds nasty," said Stew.

"It's my new favorite food," said Gus.

And then something really weird
happened. Just as we were talking about
food, I reached into the pocket of my dad's
coat and I felt something. I pulled out a
pile of packets from a Chinese restaurant.
There was some soy sauce, duck sauce, and
one hot sauce.

I showed Stew and Gus. We opened the packets and put them on our snow food. I put soy sauce on my snow pizza, Stew put duck sauce on his snow burger, and Gus put hot sauce on his snow falafel.

SNOW PIZZA WITH SOY SAUCE

SNOW BURGER WITH DUCK SAUCE

SNOW FALAFEL WITH HOT SAUCE

The sauces made the snow all different colors. The soy was brown, the duck sauce was orange, and the hot sauce was red. And all three were delicious.

"It's much better than eating *yellow* snow!" I said, and we all cracked up again.

While we were eating, I looked across the street and saw more orange snow. We walked over to see what it was.

"I hope it's duck-sauce snow," said Stew.

But it wasn't. It was fluorescent-orange spray paint. It had been used to make a big "X" on the snowbank.

"What's that for?" asked Gus.

"Duh!" I said. "X marks the spot!"

I pushed my shovel into the snow and started digging. Stew joined in with his beach shovel, and Gus pulled away piles of snow with his hands. In just a few minutes, we uncovered a fire hydrant. It wasn't as cool as treasure or anything, but it was cool enough.

Then we saw another "X" down the street and did the same thing and found another hydrant. We kept doing this until we ended up down by Wood Park.

Some man in a truck came by and saw what we were doing. "Did you boys shovel out all the hydrants?" he asked.

"Yeah," I said. "Is that okay?"

He said it was fine, thanked us, and drove on. I guess it was his job and he didn't have to do it now. After he left, we walked to the pond. It had frozen, and we wanted to check it out.

We put our feet on the edge of the ice
to see how strong it was. It didn't crack or
make any noises, so we walked on it.

Then we saw something amazing.
Trapped under the ice was this brown lumpy
shape. We got down on our hands and
knees to see what it was but couldn't figure
it out.

Then Gus was like, "Eureka! We've
found an ice man!"

Stew and I were like, "What?"

"It's a prehistoric man!" said Gus. "Sometimes they get trapped in the ice, and their bodies get all brown and dried up!"

"Oh yeah!" I said. "I saw that in a museum. Sometimes they find weapons with them."

"And sometimes," said Gus, "they still have food in their stomachs and the scientist can figure out the last meal they ate."

"Maybe he ate a woolly mammoth," I said.

"Maybe this guy ate a falafel," said Stew.

We were pressing our faces up against the ice trying to see better.

"I think his legs are down here," said Stew.

"And those are his arms," said Gus.

"What are we waiting for?" I said. "Let's dig him out and bring him to a museum."

"Yeah!" said Gus and Stew.

I started to hit the ice with my shovel. It didn't do anything. Stew tried his kiddie shovel, and it busted in half!

CRACK!

"We gotta get the ice softer before we dig. We need to melt it," I said. I got on my knees again and started rubbing the ice with my gloves. Stew got down and started to breathe on it.

"You guys don't know what you're doing," said Gus. He sat down on the ice and started rubbing his butt on it.

"The friction and heat from my butt will melt this in no time," he said.

We all got in the same position and started butt-rubbing the ice.

But our butt-rubbing wasn't melting the ice. We had to come up with a different plan. We searched around for some rocks and began scraping away at the ice.

"Make sure you don't break the ice man," said Stew.

The rocks were working well, and big chunks of ice started to crack away. Sometimes we'd get a big piece of ice and use that to crack the rest of the ice. Suddenly, this big layer of ice cracked off, and there was the ice man.

"Hmmm . . . ," I said. "It doesn't really look like a man."

"Well, they get all shriveled and stuff because they get dried out," said Stew.

"They're in the ice for a million years," said Gus.

"Did they have pockets millions of years ago?" I reached in and pulled the whole thing out at once.

It was a man's brown raincoat.

"Darn! I really thought it would be an ice man," said Stew.

Gus took it from me. "It's still pretty cool," he said, and he held it by one end. "It's as hard as a rock." The ice and water had frozen it stiff.

"It looks like a boogie board!" I said. I grabbed it from Gus, ran across the ice, tossed it down, and jumped on it. I skidded across the ice and crashed into a snowbank.

WHOOOSH!

"It's awesome!" I said.

Gus and Stew both tried the ice man boogie board. But after a few runs, it was starting to thaw and didn't work as well.

"How do you lose a coat?" I said while I was staring at it.

"Seriously," said Stew. "Was he just walking through the park and thought, 'Hey, man, I don't need my coat! I'll throw it in the pond!'?"

"Or maybe the wind blew it off him," said Gus. "He was like, 'I'm glad I got this coat because it's windy and cold,' and *whoosh*, his coat just flew away."

"Maybe he outgrew it, and was like, 'I'm too big for this coat. I think I'll leave it in the pond so someone else can use it!'" I said.

We all laughed. The coat had unraveled and was lying flat on the snow.

"This coat couldn't be too small for anyone," said Stew. He was right. It was huge.

I looked at the label. "Wow!" I said. "It's a size XXXXL2."

"That's extra, extra, extra, extra large two!" said Stew.

"Does that mean it's twice as big as an extra, extra, extra, extra large one?" asked Gus.

"I think so," I said. I picked up the top of the coat and put it on. The sleeves hung down way past my hands. Even over my dad's jacket, it was huge.

Gus and Stew got under the rest of it.

"It's like a big costume," said Gus.

"Yeah," I said. "I bet we look like a little elephant or something."

"Or a woolly mammoth," said Stew.

I pulled the shoulders of the coat up over my head. We stuck my snow shovel and Stew's broken shovel under my arms. The ends poked out from under the coat like tusks. Stew stood close behind me and wrapped his arms around me, and Gus wrapped his arms around Stew.

"You guys ready?" I asked.

They both said yes.

"Woolly attack mammoth, go!"
I screamed, and we started running. We
fell a few times, but then we got our legs
all moving at the same time. We were
getting really good at it, and could go really
fast. It must have looked awesome from
the outside.

GRRR!

"That's when you hit me with the snowball," said Ricky.

"I told you it would be a stupid story," Mean Dean said to Trent. Trent nodded.

"Anyway," said Mean Dean, "the truce is over. On the count of three, we're gonna bean you as hard as we can." He picked up a large snowball in each hand. Trent did the same.

"One," he said, "two—"

Gus and Stew jumped out from under the big coat and started hurling snowballs at Mean Dean and Trent.

"We never wait for three!" Icky Ricky said. He grabbed a snowball and joined the fight!

PARTY GAMES!

#7: Rock Star!

In your bedroom, shake talcum powder into the air and pretend to put on a smoke-filled rock concert! The person who rocks the hardest wins!

#8: Peanut Butter Freeze

Everyone strikes a pose and freezes for as long as they can. The first person to move gets beaned with peanut butter.

#9: Musical Gus Special Edition

Play loud, fast music. When the music stops, put water balloons on Gus and sit on him. Everyone wins!

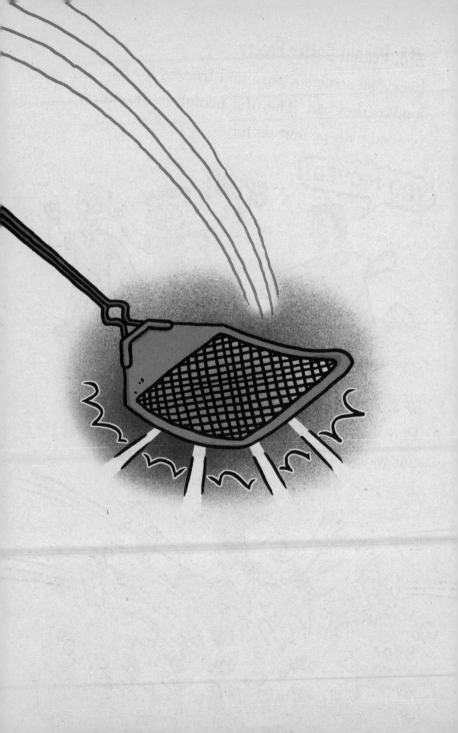

Ricky and Bruno stood in front of Bruno's parents.

"But why are you covered in a horrible mess?" asked Bruno's mom. Then she looked around the room again. "And why is that chair crooked?"

Icky Ricky continued his story.

We couldn't find the micro-stogie. We went back to the statue, and it was really looking lousy. Some of the pieces were missing, so it couldn't hold its shape.

"He looks like a guy who got nuked and is turning into a mutant," I said.

"Stop joking!" Bruno said. "If my parents see this, I'm gonna be grounded forever. It's really valuable!"

"All right!" I said. "I have another idea. Do you have any clay or something?"

"No. Why?" asked Bruno.

"We need to put something on the inside," I told him. "That way we can glue the pieces to it, and it will hold its shape."

We thought for a moment, and then I had my best idea of the day!

I took my shoe off, and then my sock. I balled the sock up and wrapped the top around the bottom. I stuffed the sock into the lower half of the statue, and it fit perfectly.

Then I started to glue the pieces onto the sock. It was like the sock was his guts. But there was one problem.

"Do you have any black paint?" I said. "My sock is white. It's going to show through all the cracks."

"No," said Bruno. "But I have another idea." He ran off and came back with a little round tin can.

"Shoe polish," he said as he handed it to me. I opened it up, and it was black and almost like paint. Then he handed me a long, thin paintbrush.

"Here! I got this, too," he said. "My
mom uses it to dust in really small places."

I put some shoe polish on the brush
and started to fill in the cracks. A fly
landed on the statue and I brushed it away.

"Aaaagh!" screamed Bruno. "That
stupid fly is back!" He picked up the
flyswatter and tried to hit it. He fell over
the coffee table, and his hand landed right
on the glue tube.

Glue shot like a rocket from the tip of the tube. It was going to hit the wall, but I jumped forward and the glue shot all over my shirt. None of it got anywhere in the room.

SPLAT!

"That was close!" I said. I put the paintbrush down on the edge of the table. The fly landed on it.

Whap! Bruno hit the edge of the brush and it went sailing. It flew toward the wall, but I dove across the table and blocked it. Then I rolled on the ground, and the glue on my shirt picked up the newspapers we had put on the floor.

The fly landed in the open shoe polish
can. *Whap!* Bruno hit the can hard, but the
fly got away.

It landed on the clock.

"Aaaagh!" said Bruno. "My parents are
going to be home any minute! We gotta
clean all this up!"

"Okay!" I said. I grabbed all the
newspapers and balled them up tight.
Bruno closed the shoe polish and grabbed
the brush and ran off to put them away. I
stuffed everything into the trash bag Bruno
had wanted me to wear. I found the glue
cap and tube and chucked them in also.

Bruno came back in. "The room looks
perfect," he said, "except for the statue."

The fly landed on my face!

Bruno smacked me right in the face
and left a big black spot of shoe polish.
Then the front door opened, and that's
when you came in.

"I'm sorry, Mom and Dad!" said Bruno.
"It's my fault. Ricky did everything he could
to help, but we couldn't fix it."

They all looked at the pathetic
sculpture. The pieces weren't lined up.
It had black polish smeared all over it.
The hands were backward, and it was
starting to sag. It was really awful.

"I'm sorry," said Ricky. "I tried my best."

"Well," said Bruno's mom, "you two need to get busy with your book report."

"Yeah," said Ricky.

"Okay," said Bruno.

The fly buzzed between the boys and Bruno's parents.

"It's back!" shouted Bruno, and he started swinging the swatter all over. Bruno's parents ran from the room and were back in no time. His mom had her own swatter, and his dad had some paper towels and cleaning spray. *Wham! Bam! Crash!* Bruno and his mom swung and swatted and missed and swatted again. Bruno's dad sprayed every spot where the fly had landed and scrubbed it clean in a frenzy.

Finally the fly landed on the statue again and Bruno swung hard. He hit the statue, sending it sailing off the coffee table right into the garbage bag.

Bruno gasped! "I'm sorry!" he said.

"That's okay," said Bruno's dad. He looked at Bruno's mom. "That's a shame, dear. I know that was a special statue to you."

"Me?" said Bruno's mom. "I thought you liked it. I always thought it was hideous."

"Really?" said Bruno's dad. "I think it's hideous, too. I never said anything because I assumed you loved it."

"Nope," said Bruno's mom.

"But isn't it valuable?" asked Bruno. "Isn't it really old?"

"Nah," said his mother. "I think your grandma won it at a bowling alley in Hackensack."

The fly landed on the shelf where the bowler dude had originally been. Bruno swatted it quickly.

"Got it!" he shouted. He lifted the swatter, and on the shelf there was a little green-and-black glob that had once been a fly.

"Quick!" shouted Bruno's mother. "Clean it before it leaves a stain!"

ICKY·RICKY 6

THE BACKPACK AQUARIUM